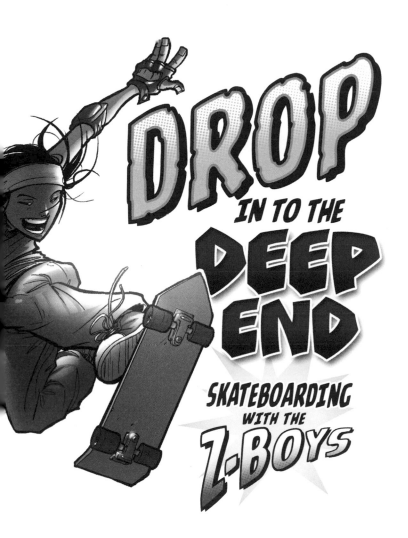

# DROP
## IN TO THE
# DEEP END

## SKATEBOARDING
### WITH THE
# Z-BOYS

### STONE ARCH BOOKS
MINNEAPOLIS   SAN DIEGO

# DROP IN TO THE DEEP END

WRITTEN BY *XAVIER NIZ*

ILLUSTRATED BY *PONXLAB'S*
LINEART *JESUS ABURTO*
COLOR *MAESE FARES*

DESIGNER: *BRANN GARVEY*

EDITOR: *DONALD LEMKE*

ASSOC. EDITOR: *SEAN TULIEN*

ART DIRECTOR: *BOB LENTZ*

CREATIVE DIRECTOR: *HEATHER KINDSETH*

EDITORIAL DIRECTOR: *MICHAEL DAHL*

Graphic Flash is published by Stone Arch Books, 151 Good Counsel Drive, P.O. Box 669, Mankato, Minnesota 56002
www.stonearchbooks.com Copyright © 2009 by Stone Arch Books. All rights reserved. No part of this publication may be
reproduced in whole or in part, or stored in a retrieval system, or transmitted in any form or by any means, electronic,
mechanical, photocopying, recording, or otherwise, without written permission of the publisher.

Library of Congress Cataloging-in-Publication Data

Niz, Xavier.
 Drop in to the deep end : skateboarding with the Z-Boys / by Xavier W. Niz ; illustrated by Jesus Aburto.
    p. cm. -- (Graphic Flash)
 ISBN 978-1-4342-1581-9 (lib. bdg.)
 [1. Skateboarding--Fiction.] I. Aburto, Jesus, ill. II. Title.
 PZ7.N653Dr 2010
 [Fic]--dc22                        2009013562

Summary: In the late 1970s, Skip Jenson just moved from California to a small town in Ohio. Although he doesn't fit in at
first, the fifteen-year-old soon finds other students at Wilbur Wright Middle School who share his passion, skateboarding.
Although Skip is psyched to ride with a new crowd, he isn't ready to adopt their rebellious ways. Now this California kid must
show his new friends the new way to ride.

Printed in the United States of America

# CONTENTS

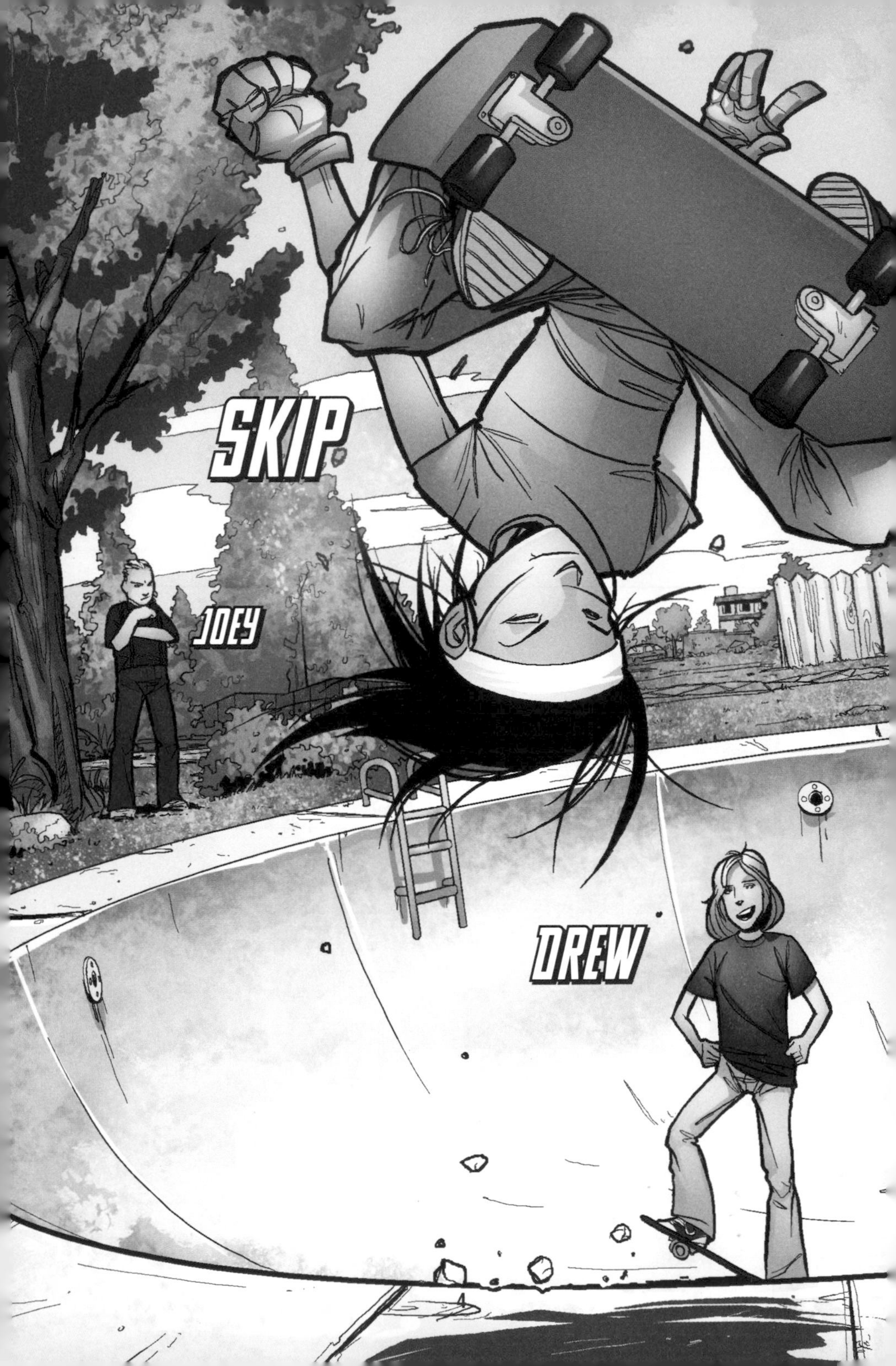
SKIP
JOEY
DREW

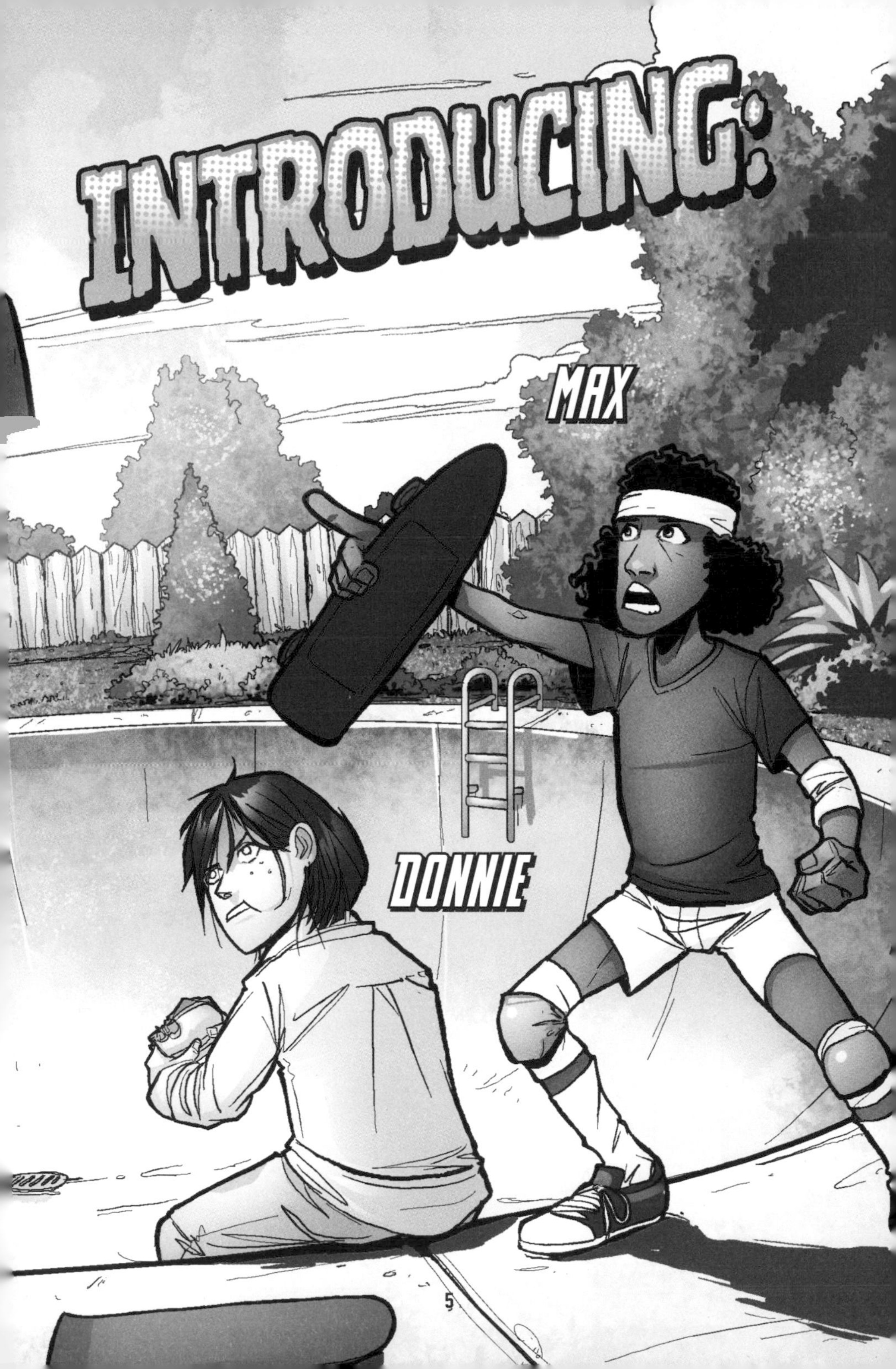
INTRODUCING:
MAX
DONNIE

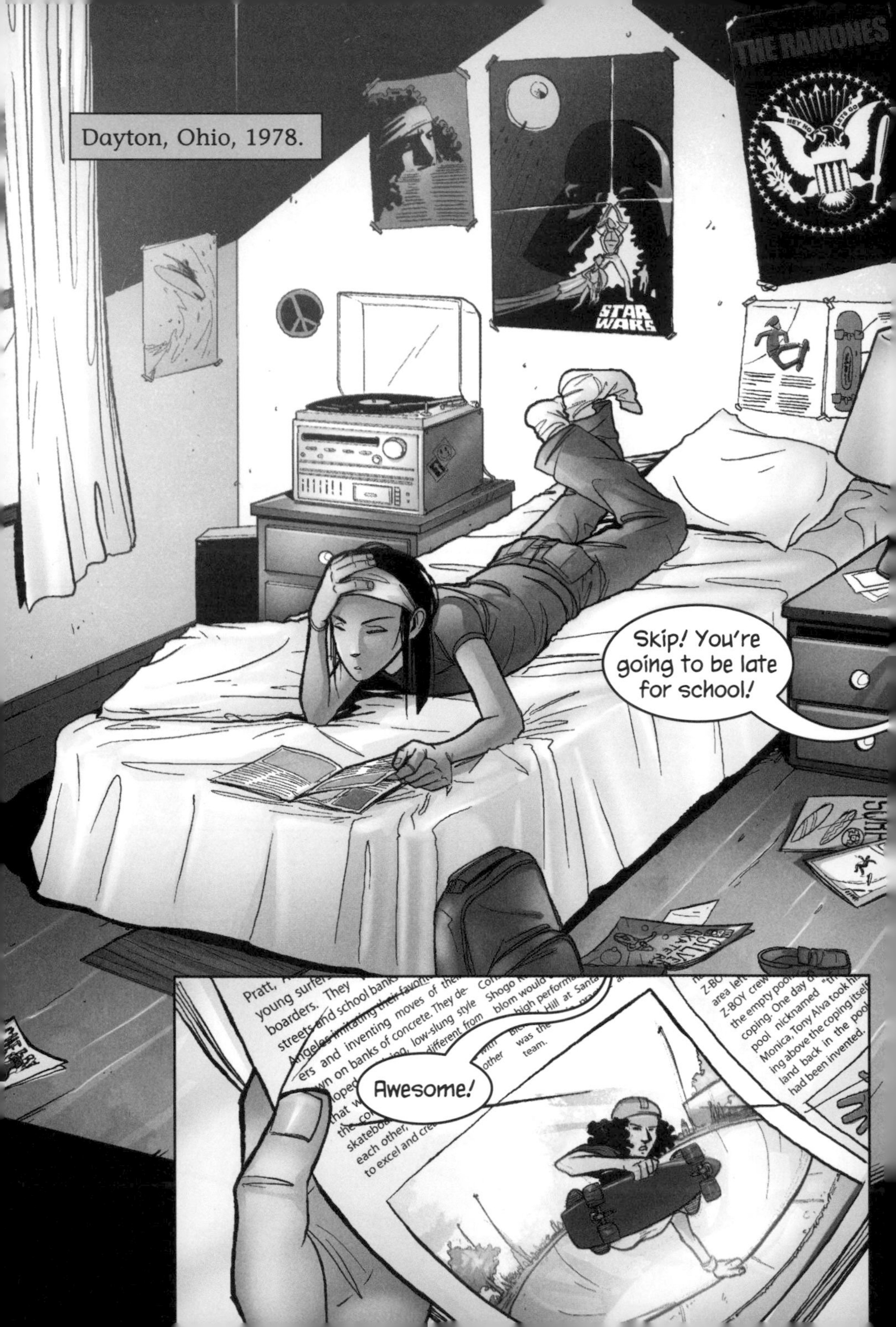
Dayton, Ohio, 1978.
THE RAMONES
STAR WARS
Skip! You're going to be late for school!
Awesome!

# CHAPTER 1

# NEW KID IN TOWN

Skip didn't hear his mother calling from downstairs. His Ramones record was playing too loudly in his room. Not that he would have heard her anyway. Skip's attention was focused on the pages of the latest issue of *SkateBoarder* magazine. Skip flipped the pages slowly. He was lost among the photographs of his heroes, the Z-Boys, performing their newest skating tricks.

"Skip!" his mother yelled again.

Skip turned another page and stared in disbelief at the photo. It was a photo of Tony Alva, one hand gripping the lip of a drained pool, the other holding onto the edge of his board.

Skip daydreamed of being back in California.

A drought had hit his former home in Santa Monica, California. All of the swimming pools were empty because of a water shortage. He used to spend all day practicing the moves that he saw the Z-Boys do in the big, empty swimming pools.

"Skip Wilson Archer!" Skip's mother said. "Didn't you hear me yelling your name?"

Skip looked up to see his mother standing in the doorway of his room. She looked very annoyed. She walked over to the record player and lifted the needle off of his Ramones album.

"You know I don't like it when you play this kind of music so loud," she said. "The neighbors have already complained."

"Um, yeah, sorry," Skip answered. He rolled up his magazine and shoved it into his back pocket.

"Honey, look," Skip's mom said, her tone changing from anger to concern.

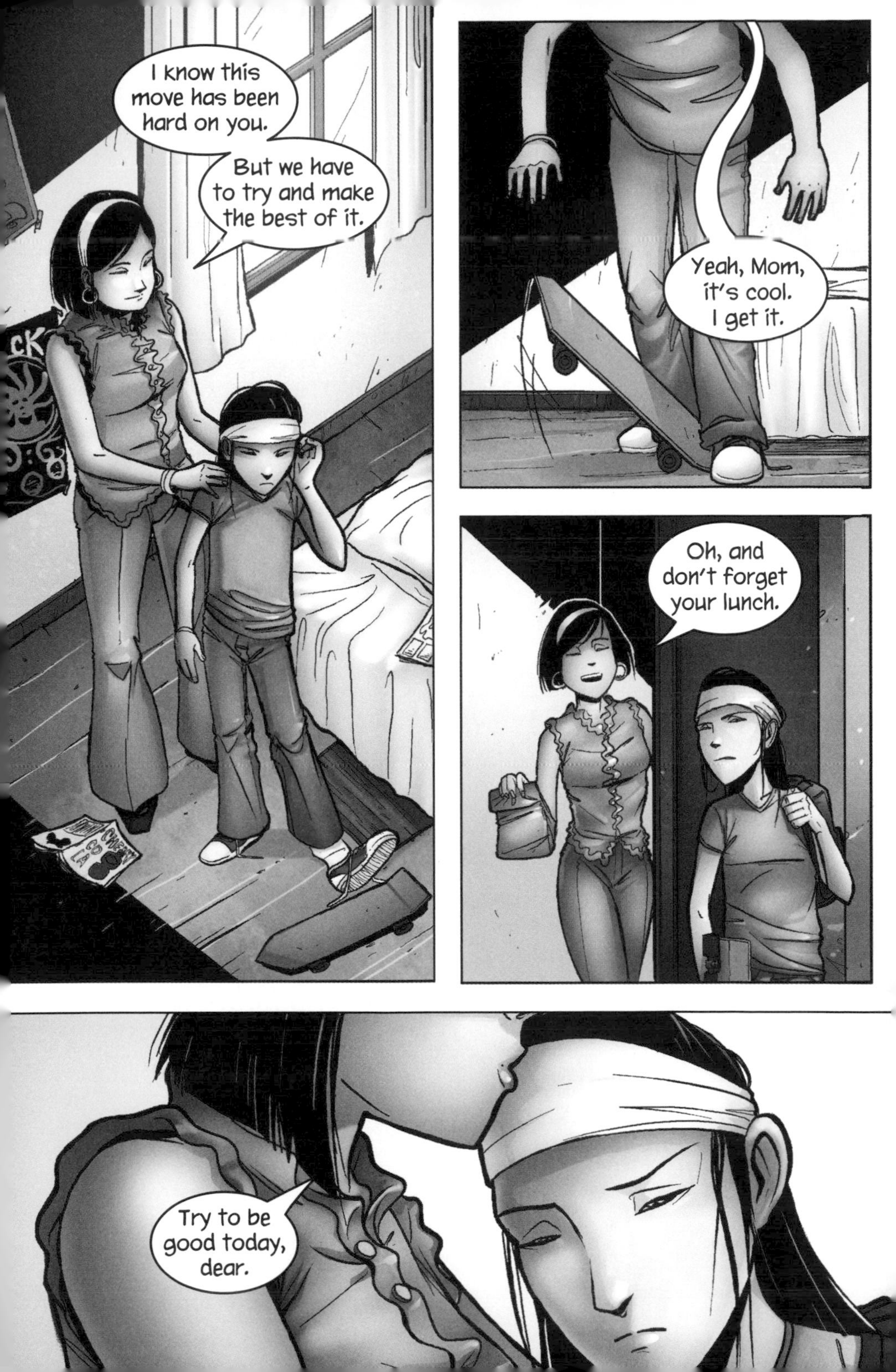
I know this move has been hard on you.
But we have to try and make the best of it.
Yeah, Mom, it's cool. I get it.
Oh, and don't forget your lunch.
Try to be good today, dear.

Out on the street, Skip kicked hard behind his skateboard. His new house sat at the bottom of a steep hill. It was so steep that it would be simpler just to walk to the top. But Skip never walked anywhere if he could skate there instead.

At the top of the hill, Skip paused for a moment before tearing down the other side. As he picked up speed, Skip crouched lower and lower on his board. Soon, he was almost sitting on top of it. This position reduced his drag and helped him steer his board at high speeds. Skip liked to go fast. The faster the better, in his opinion.

Back in California, he and his friends used to skate hills all the time. Skip missed his friends. He missed his old school. He'd been in Dayton, Ohio, for almost a month, and the city still didn't feel like home. He hadn't made any friends, and no one liked him. Skip tried not to think too much about his old life as he sped down the hill.

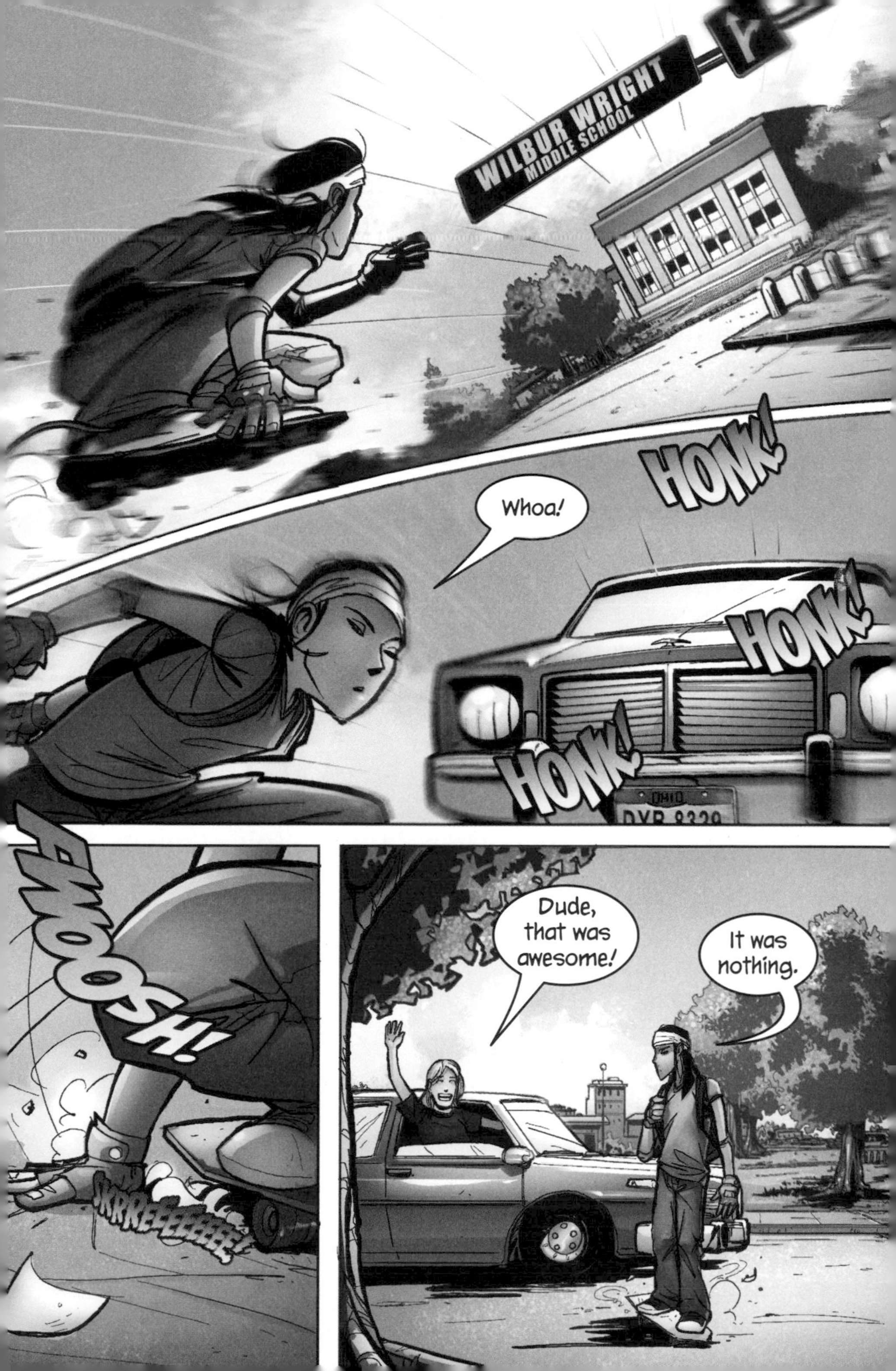
WILBUR WRIGHT
MIDDLE SCHOOL
Whoa!
HONK!
HONK!
HONK!
FWOOSH!
SKRREEEEEEEEE!
Dude, that was awesome!
It was nothing.

"You could have been seriously hurt," an older man said, poking his head out the driver's side car window. "Honestly, I can't believe skateboards are still legal."

Skip watched the car pull away. The kid that got dropped off walked toward him. "My dad doesn't like skateboarding," said the kid.

"I got that," Skip replied, grinning.

"Anyway, that move looked like a heel drag into a 360," the kid said.

"It was! You skate?" Skip asked.

"Yeah. My name's Drew," the kid said. "You're the new kid, right?"

"The name's Skip," Skip replied.

"Well, Skip," said Drew, "my friends and I are going riding after school today. Want to join us?"

"Yeah, why not," Skip said with a smile.

# CHAPTER 2

Skip found Drew practicing 360s in the rear parking lot after school. Skip watched his new friend unsuccessfully try to link two of them together. Instead, he ended up flinging himself to the ground.

"Hey," Skip said while Drew dusted himself off. "Were you trying to do a 720?"

"Yeah," Drew replied, "but I can't seem to get the last rotation right."

"You have to build up more speed before you start the turn," Skip told him. "Then really twist your upper body. Don't worry about the rest. Your feet will just follow."

"Thanks, man," Drew said. "I'll try that."

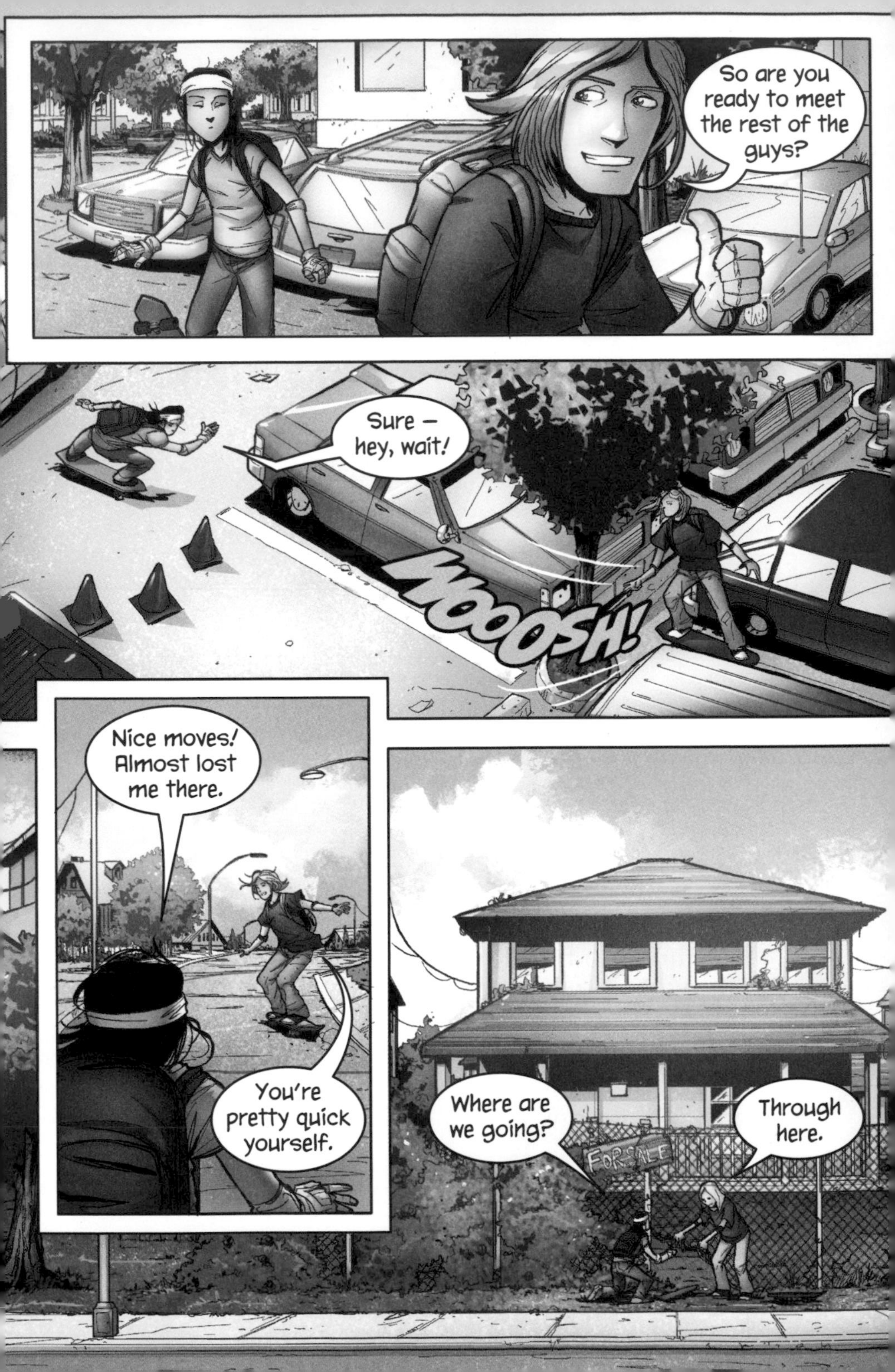
So are you ready to meet the rest of the guys?
Sure — hey, wait!
WOOOSH!
Nice moves! Almost lost me there.
You're pretty quick yourself.
Where are we going?
Through here.
FOR SALE

Skip got on all fours and crawled through the space Drew found in the fence. They were standing in front of a large two-story house. It had a huge, empty pool in back.

"What is this place?" Skip asked Drew.

"The owners moved out a couple of weeks ago," Drew said. "My dad's a real estate agent, and he's trying to sell it for them."

"It's nice," Skip said.

"The owners were kind enough to drain the pool before they left," Drew added. "I guess they didn't want the filters to get clogged or something. Come on, let me introduce you to the boys."

Drew walked over to his friends and sat down next to them.

"Hey, guys! This is Skip Archer," he told them, pointing over his shoulder. "He's new in town. Skip, this is Max Samuels and Donnie Heinz."

Drew added, "Oh, and the kid about to drop in to the pool is Tony, Max's younger brother."

Max and Donnie didn't look up at Skip. They were focused on what was happening below them. Skip walked over to the edge of the pool just in time to see a young boy riding his skateboard into the bottom.

"So, you skate?" Max asked. He still hadn't looked up at Skip.

"Yeah," Skip replied.

"Ever skate a bowl like this?" asked Donnie, pointing at the empty pool.

"Once or twice," Skip answered.

Max stood and looked Skip directly in his eyes. "Then show us what you can do!" he said.

Skip was happy to accept Max's challenge. He had dropped in to empty pools a thousand times.

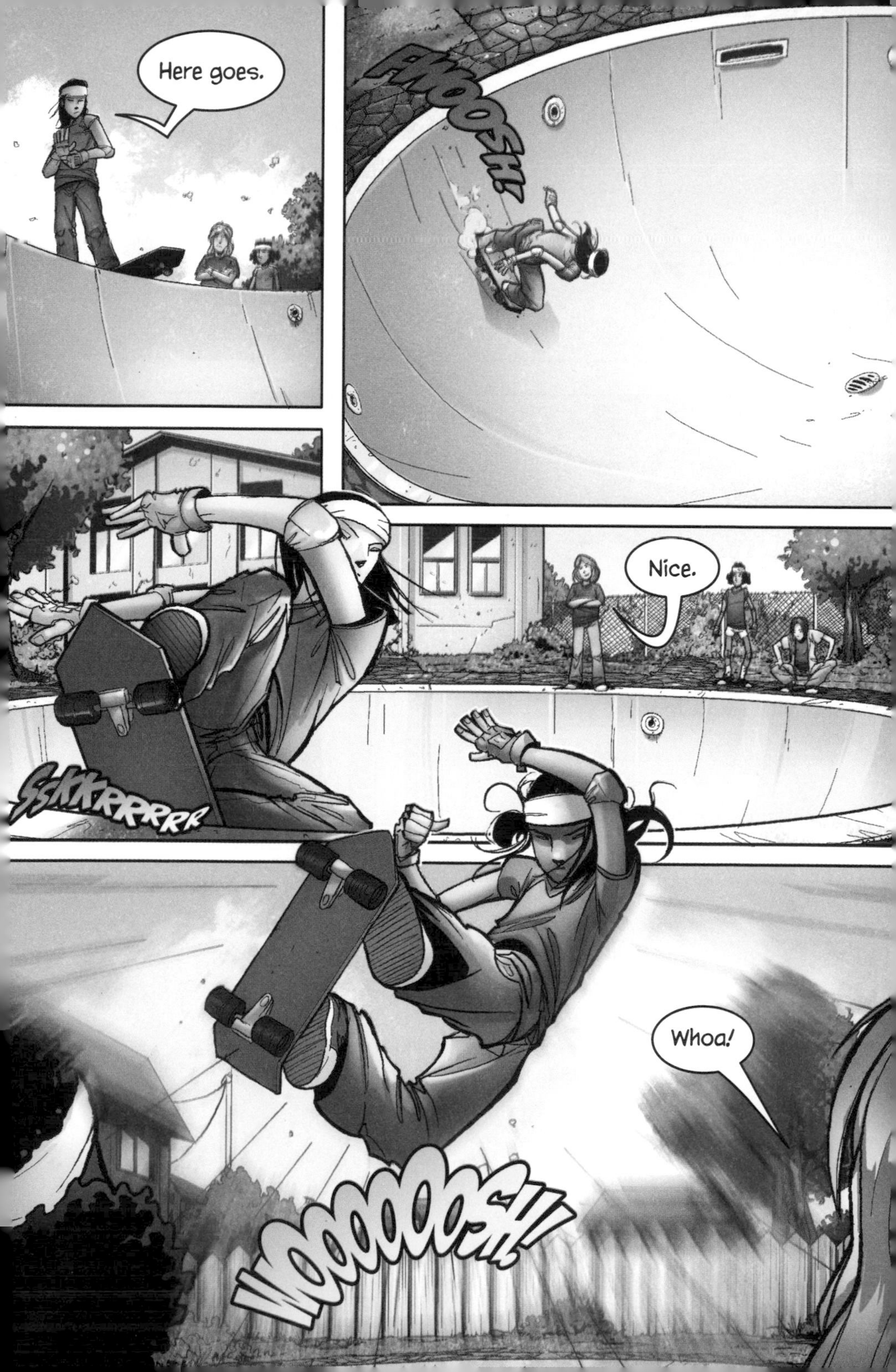
Here goes.
FWOOSH!
Nice.
SSKKRRRRR
Whoa!
WOOOOOOSH!

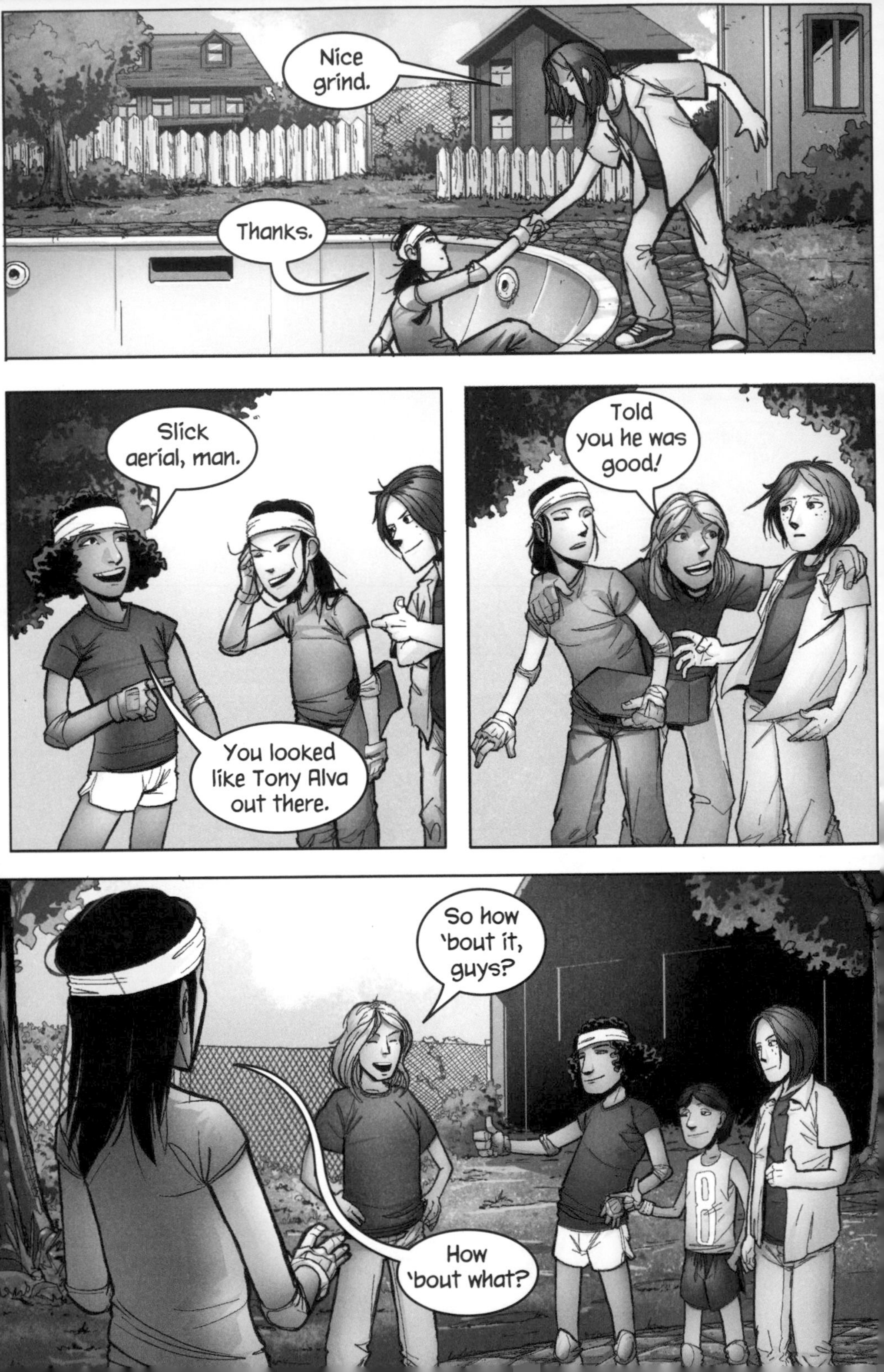
Nice grind.
Thanks.
Slick aerial, man.
You looked like Tony Alva out there.
Told you he was good!
So how 'bout it, guys?
How 'bout what?

"Here's the deal," Drew said to Skip. "There's a regional skating tournament coming up soon. We got a local sports store to sponsor us. Donnie, Max, Tony, and I are on the team. But Tony's too young to enter. So, we need a fourth member."

Drew leaned in close to Skip's face. "Are you interested?" Drew asked.

Skip had never skated in a tournament before, but he had watched several back in California. He paused for a moment before answering.

"Sure," he said. "Sounds like fun."

"Cool!" Drew replied. He was clearly happy that Skip had accepted their offer. "We'll meet up after school tomorrow and start practicing."

# CHAPTER 3

# A FEW NEW TRICKS

The next day, Drew and Donnie were waiting for Skip after school. They were trying on black t-shirts that had "Dayton Sports" emblazoned on the front in large gold lettering.

As Skip walked up to them, Drew pulled off the black shirt and exchanged it for a regular one in his bag. "Check this out," Drew said, handing Skip the black shirt.

"What are they?" Skip asked.

"Team uniforms," Donnie answered. "Hold it up. Let's see how it looks."

Skip looked down at the golden logo held over his chest. He felt a little silly, but he also felt proud. He had never belonged to a team before.

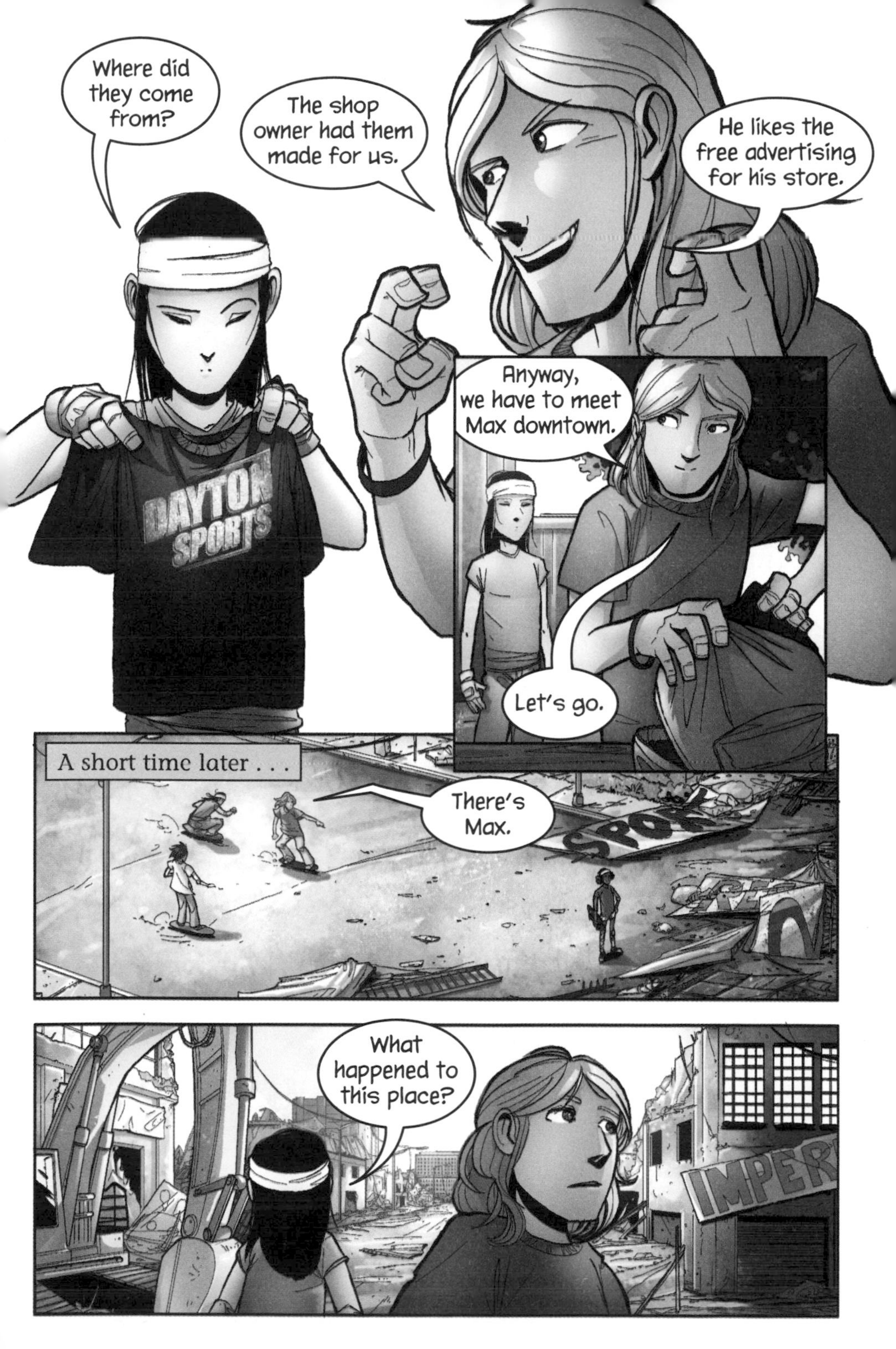
Where did they come from?
The shop owner had them made for us.
He likes the free advertising for his store.
DAYTON SPORTS
Anyway, we have to meet Max downtown.
Let's go.
A short time later . . .
There's Max.
What happened to this place?
IMPER

"Weird, huh?" Drew said. "A tornado came through here last year and wrecked most of the buildings. They're supposed to be tearing them down, but that hasn't happened yet. In the meantime, the area has lots of asphalt and no traffic. It's the perfect place to practice!"

"Let's get started!" Max said. "Did you bring the cups, Drew?"

"They're right here," Drew answered. He dug into his bag and pulled out a stack of paper cups. Then he started to place the cups on a small hill in a straight line.

"Come on," Drew said. He slapped Skip on the back. "We'll show you how it's done!"

Drew hopped on his board and sped through the course. Max and Donnie followed.

After the first few runs, Tony moved the cups closer and closer together.

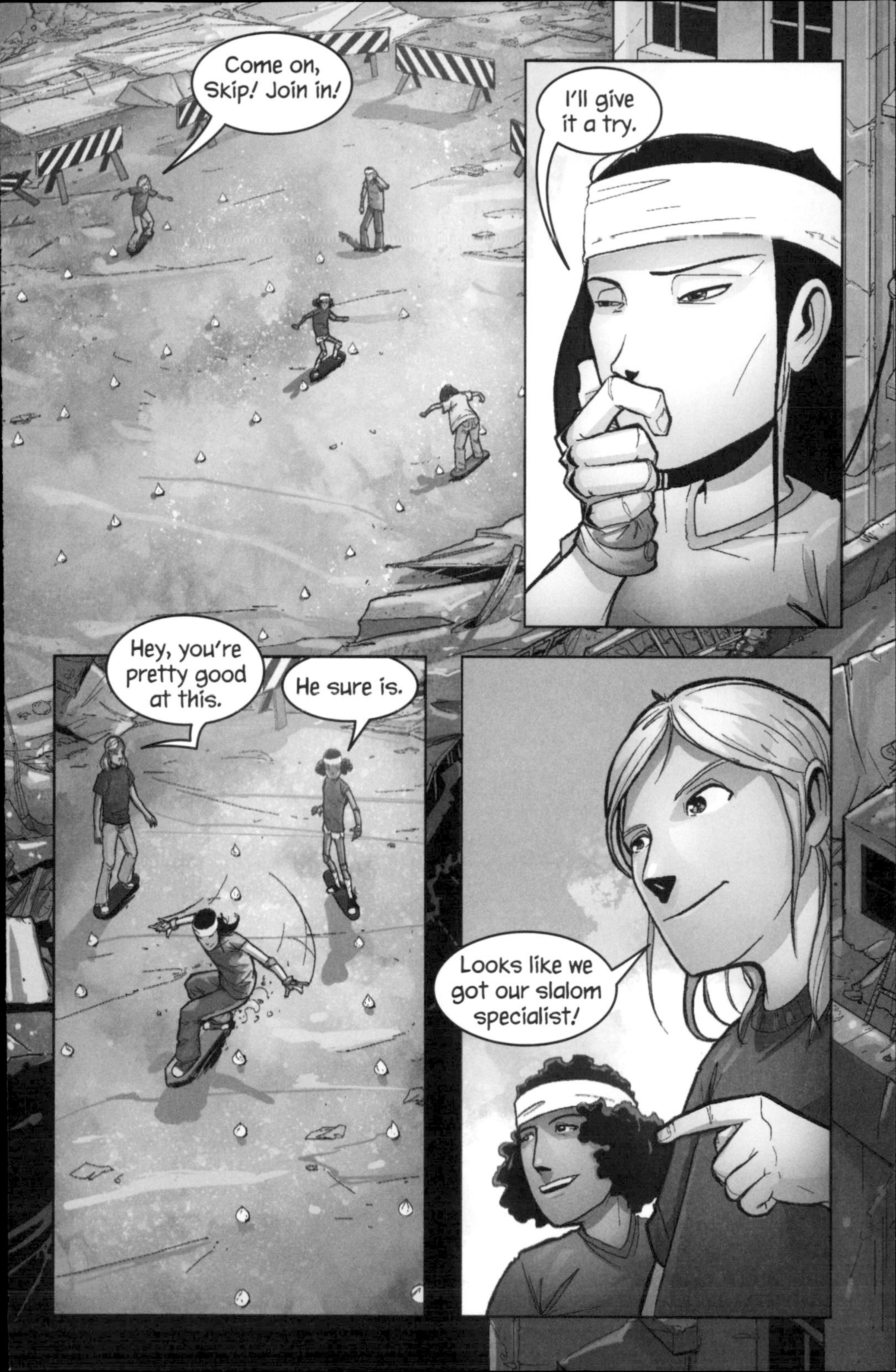

Come on, Skip! Join in!
I'll give it a try.
Hey, you're pretty good at this.
He sure is.
Looks like we got our slalom specialist!

"How did you learn to get low like that?" Donnie asked Skip. "You look like Tony Alva, the way you hunch down on your board."

"Really?" Skip asked, flattered to be compared again to his skating idol. "I'm not sure. It just feels natural. A lot of the guys I know from California skate this way. It probably comes from all the surfing we do."

"Well, I don't care where it comes from," Drew said. "If it makes me half as fast as you, I'm willing to try it."

Drew got on his board. He kicked hard to build up speed. Then, he tried to sit as low as Skip had been. After a few feet, he fell off his board.

"I'm sure you'll get it eventually," Skip said, helping Drew off the ground.

"Maybe," Drew said. "In the meantime, let's practice our freestyle routines. You're up, Max!"

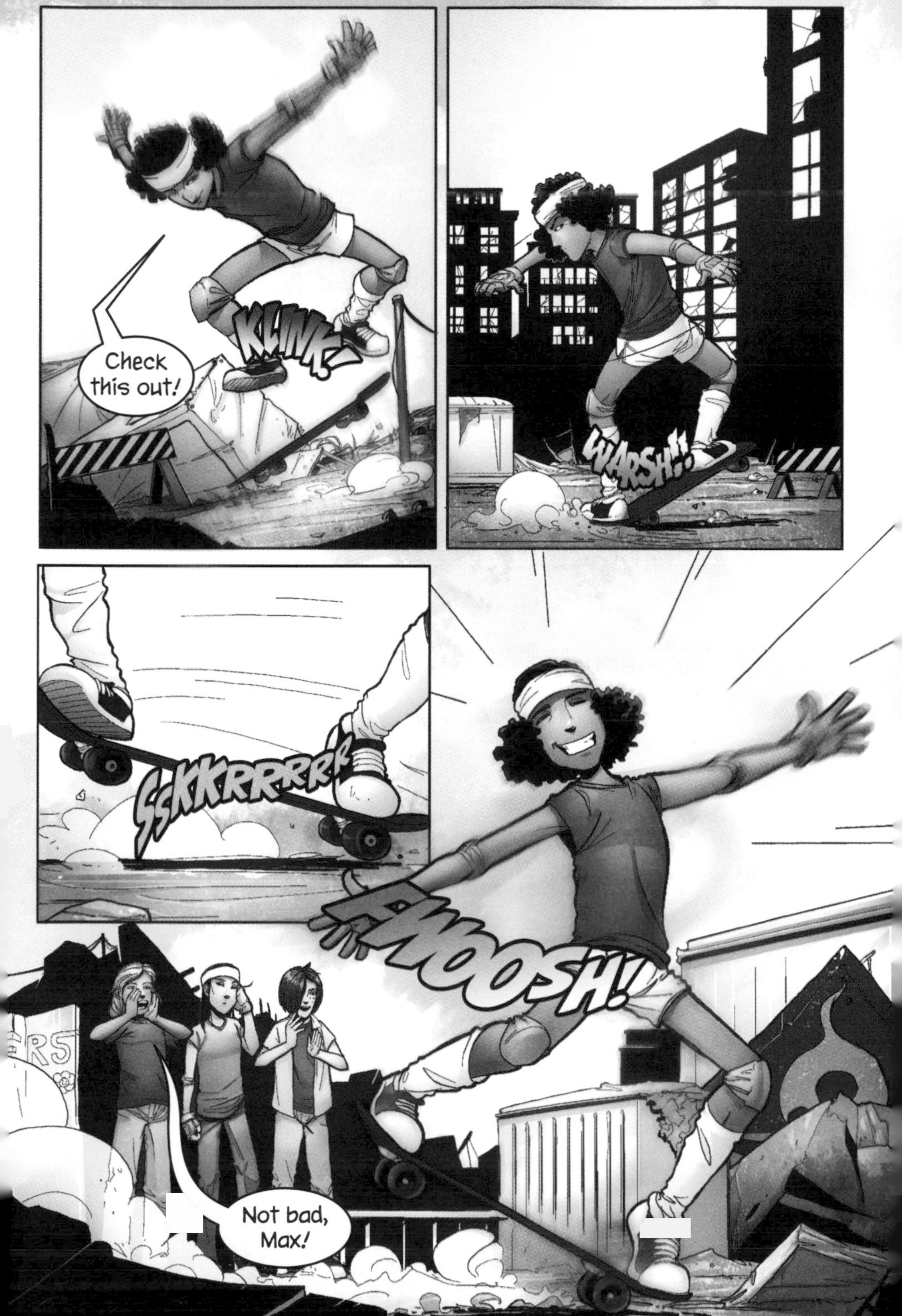
Check this out!
KLINK!
WARSH!!
SSKKRRRRRR
WHOOSH!
Not bad, Max!

"So, what do you think?" Max asked Skip as he jumped off his board.

Skip looked at his new friend and tried not to laugh. "Not bad at all," he said. "But don't you think those tricks are a little old? Skaters have been doing End-Overs for years."

"So?" Max replied, a little offended. "They're difficult to do!"

"Yeah, man," Drew interrupted. "Those are high-scoring tricks. They're classics!"

"Yeah, they're classics all right," Skip said. "But they're boring, too. Don't you want to do something new? Something that'll knock their socks off?"

"Like what?" Max asked.

"Like this," Skip said, grabbing his board. He sped in a straight line right toward a half-broken brick wall.

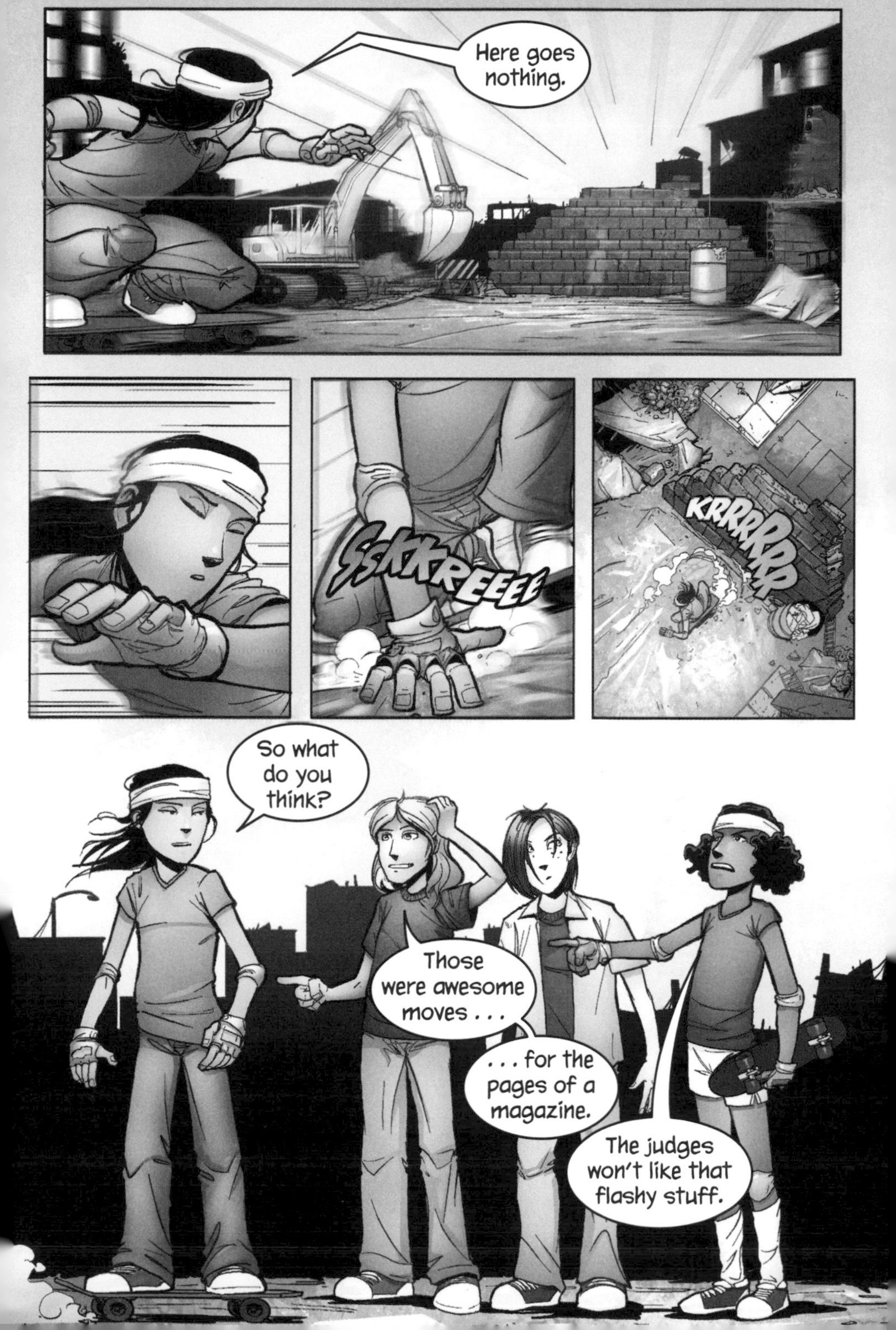
Here goes nothing.
SSKKREEEEE
KRRRRRRR
So what do you think?
Those were awesome moves . . .
. . . for the pages of a magazine.
The judges won't like that flashy stuff.

When Skip turned around, he saw a group of older kids. They were on skateboards, heading straight toward him.

"Losers!" one kid yelled.

"Get out of here!" said another kid.

"Run!" Drew yelled.

Skip jumped on his board and took off. The boys skated as fast as they could through the streets. After several blocks, they stopped.

"Who were they?" Skip asked, exhausted.

"The Eagles," Donnie answered. "A gang from Belmont High School. Trust me, you don't want to cross paths with them."

"Last year they took Tony's board and beat me up when I tried to stop them," Max added.

"Best thing to do when you see an Eagle," Drew added, "is *run!*"

CHAPTER 4

# THE EAGLES

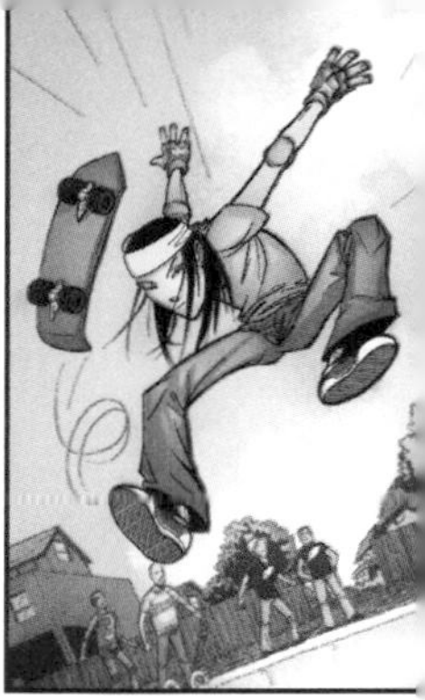

The next day, Skip and his friends returned to the construction zone. Despite their run-in with the Eagles, it was still the best place to practice their routines. As a precaution, they each took turns standing at the top of the hill while the other boys skated below. That way, they could see if the Eagles were coming.

The boys practiced every day for the next two weeks. Skip spent the entire time focusing on his slalom skills. He became faster and faster, until the rest of the team couldn't keep up. By the end of the second week, Skip was beginning to think that he might have a shot at winning the tournament. As far as the race was concerned, Skip liked his team's chances.

Skip was not as confident about the freestyle part of the competition. The boys still hadn't settled their argument about what tricks to use for their routines. Max, Donnie, and Drew all refused to use any of the tricks that Skip suggested. Skip refused to do a freestyle routine unless he could do it his way. The boys couldn't seem to come to an agreement.

One day, Skip was working on his own freestyle tricks alone. He was so focused on getting his hand plant right that he didn't notice someone had walked up behind him. He nearly jumped out of his skin when he felt a hand reach down and grab his shoulder. Then he realized that the hand belonged to one of the Eagles.

"Hey," the older teenage boy said, not letting go of Skip's shirt.

Skip looked up at the big kid and swallowed.

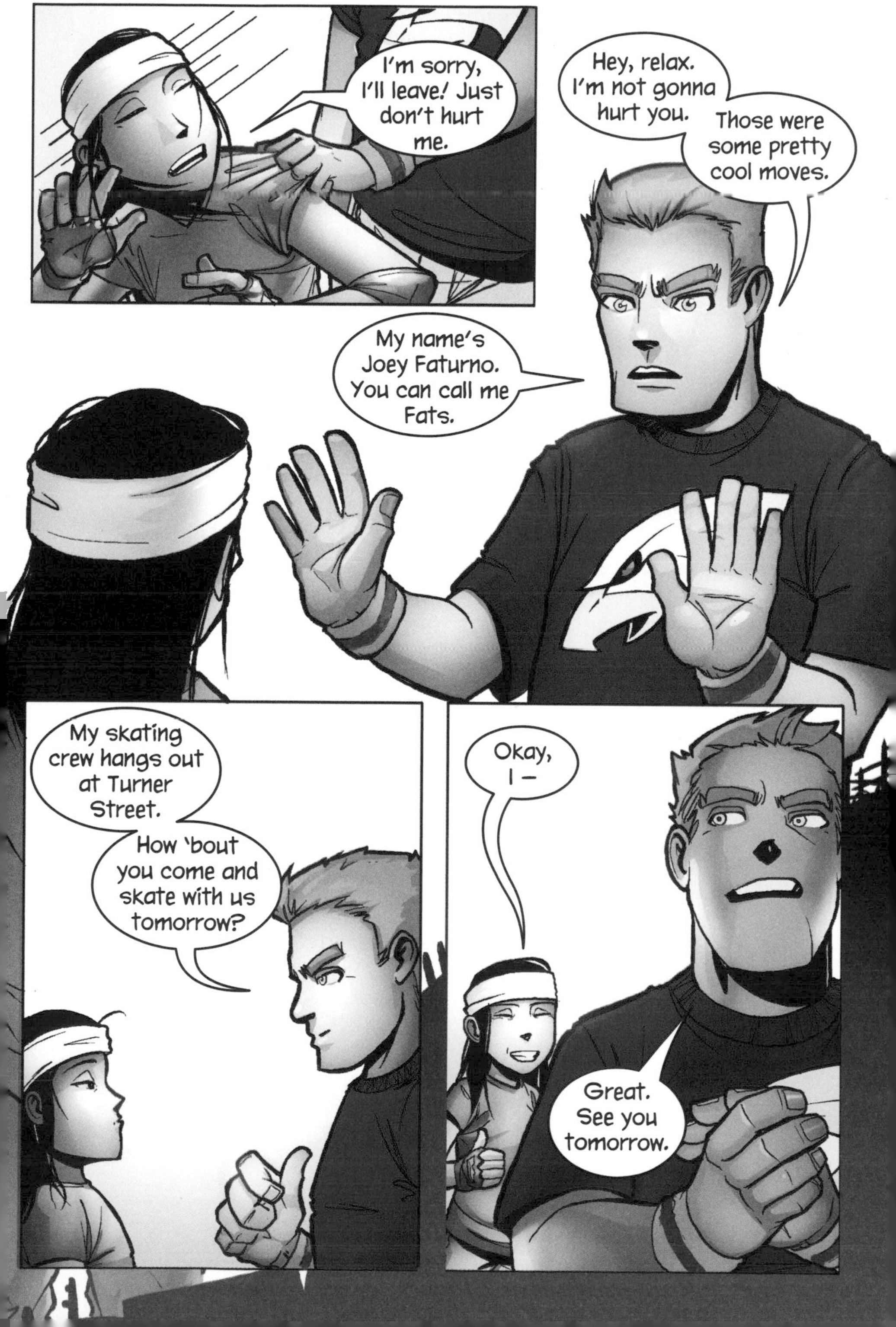
I'm sorry, I'll leave! Just don't hurt me.
Hey, relax. I'm not gonna hurt you.
Those were some pretty cool moves.
My name's Joey Faturno. You can call me Fats.
My skating crew hangs out at Turner Street.
How 'bout you come and skate with us tomorrow?
Okay, I —
Great. See you tomorrow.

Skip was as confused as he was excited. He had been invited to skate with the Eagles! But he wasn't sure if he should feel flattered or worried.

The next day, Skip went straight to Turner Street after school. He was nervous about hanging out with Joey and his friends, but he knew he couldn't turn them down. Skip found a small hole in the chain-link fence that lined the edge of the street. As he slid down the concrete embankment, he saw a large group of teenagers hanging out by the pool. Cautiously, he walked toward them, looking for Joey in the crowd.

"There's my guy," Joey yelled, seeing Skip.

"Hey," Skip replied.

"I was just telling the rest of the crew about your moves," Joey said.

"Yeah, Fats says that you're a real all-star," a tall kid said.

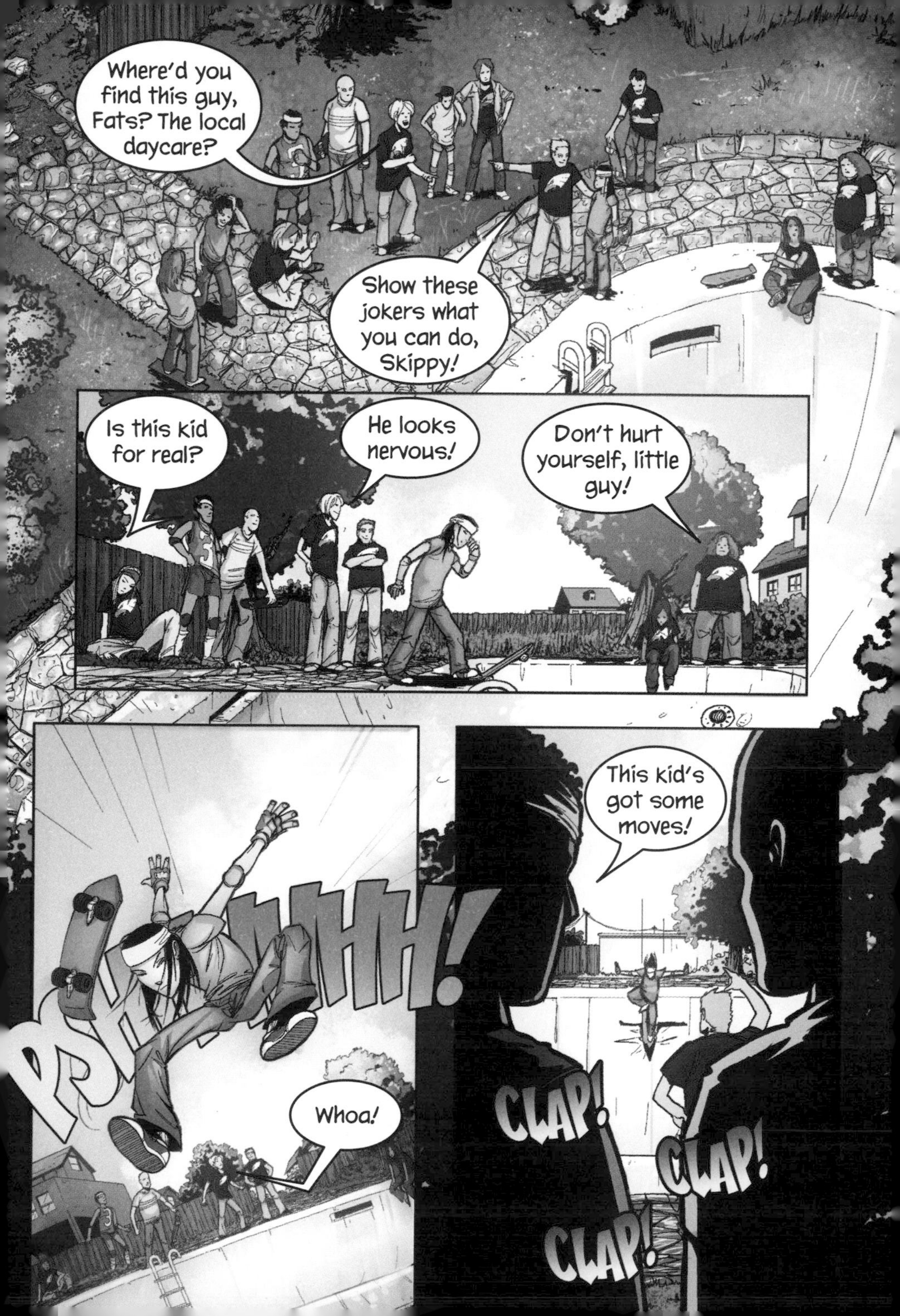
Where'd you find this guy, Fats? The local daycare?
Show these jokers what you can do, Skippy!
Is this kid for real?
He looks nervous!
Don't hurt yourself, little guy!
PSHHHH!
Whoa!
This kid's got some moves!
CLAP!
CLAP!
CLAP!

Next Skip skated along the slope and wove back and forth like he was on a slalom course. His weaving got tighter and tighter. On his last pass, he turned into a kick slide. He did a few more flashy tricks for the crowd. They loved every one of them.

"Not bad, Skippy," Joey said as Skip climbed out of the pool. "That was a pretty sweet run."

"Nice moves, kid," an older boy said to him.

"It was nothing," Skip said, trying to be cool.

"Yeah, right," Joey said. "Anyway, that was some nice skating. Can you show me how you do those turns?"

Skip was flattered. "Of course," he said.

Skip spent the rest of the day hanging out by the pool and teaching the Eagles how to do his tricks. For the first time since leaving California, Skip felt like he really belonged.

# CHAPTER 5

# STUCK ON THE SIDELINES

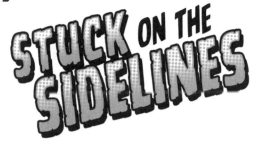

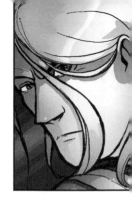

Over the next week, Skip spent most of his free time hanging out with Joey Fats and the rest of the Eagles. Every day they went down to the river and skated the steep slopes of the concrete banks. Skip had even started teaching the gang his low style of riding and all the tricks he knew. Skip was happy to show them. Deep down, he was starting to feel like an Eagle.

With so much of his time devoted to his new friends, Skip had stopped practicing with Drew and the rest of the Dayton Sports team. He felt bad about abandoning them, but he was bored with all of the arguing and fighting. If they wanted to use their old-fashioned tricks, then so be it. Skip was happy to spend his time with people who could appreciate his new style.

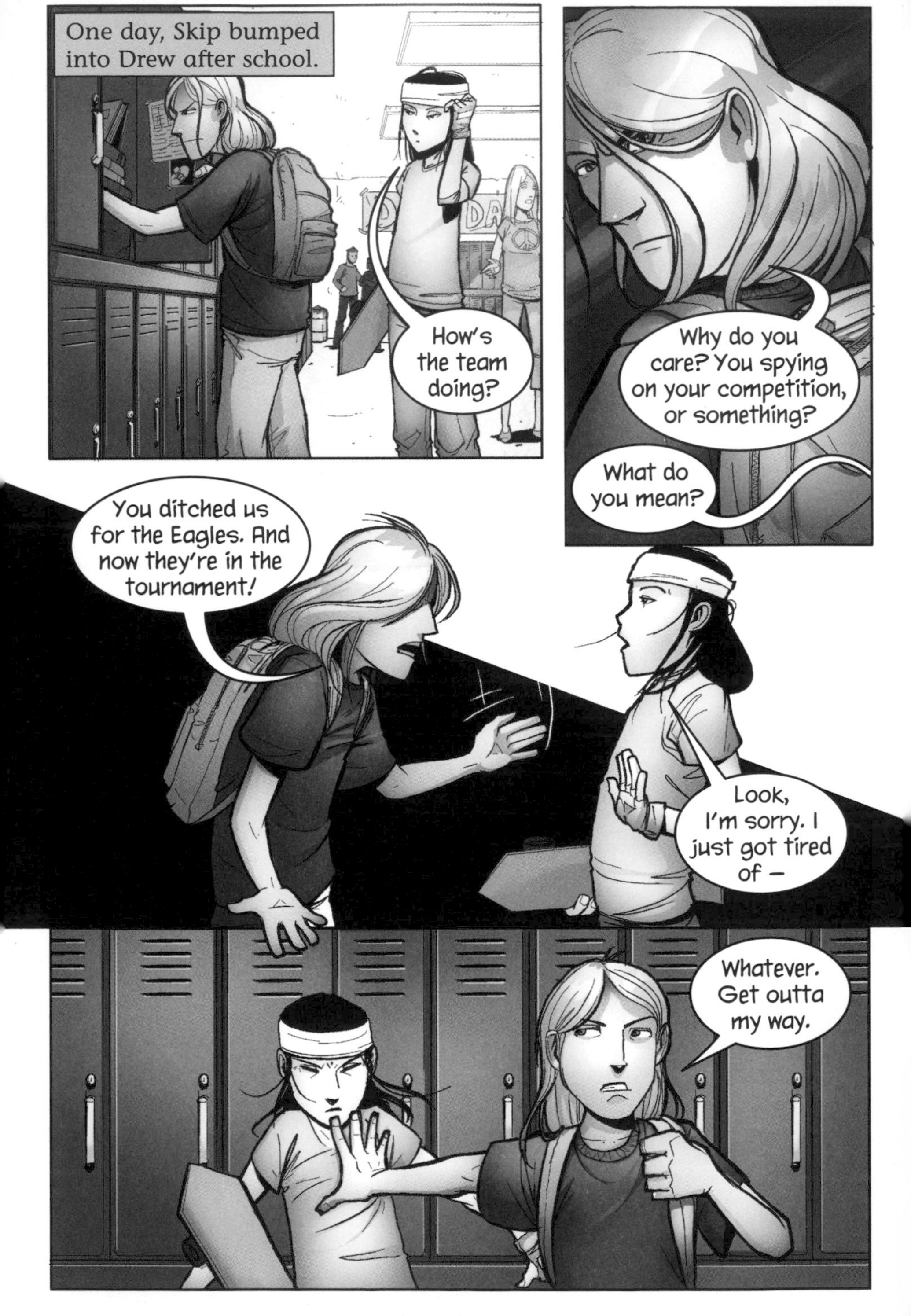
One day, Skip bumped into Drew after school.
How's the team doing?
Why do you care? You spying on your competition, or something?
What do you mean?
You ditched us for the Eagles. And now they're in the tournament!
Look, I'm sorry. I just got tired of –
Whatever. Get outta my way.

Skip didn't know anything about the Eagles skating in regionals. As far as he knew, they hadn't even heard of the tournament. The encounter with Drew made Skip feel very uneasy.

*Drew can believe what he wants,* Skip thought as he left school.

When Skip got to Turner Street, he saw all of the Eagles gathered around in a crowd. As he approached them, he noticed that Joey was handing out red shirts with the word "Eagles" printed on the back. Skip slipped through the group of the kids to the middle.

"What are those?" he asked.

"What, these?" Joey smiled, pretending to be clueless. "Aren't they cool? We're going to wear them to the competition next week, of course."

"The competition?" Skip asked. "So you *are* competing in the skating tournament?

"Yeah, man," Joey said. "We've been practicing all the tricks you taught us. You're a really good coach, Skippy."

"Coach?" Skip asked, trying to make sense of what Fats was saying.

"Sure," said Joey. "In fact, you should come to the competition. You can watch from the sidelines as we blow everyone else out of the water."

"Watch from the sidelines?" Skip asked. "You mean, I'm not on the team?"

"On the team?" Joey said, chuckling. "Sorry, kid. You're a good skater, but only Eagles can skate on our team."

Skip couldn't believe it. The Eagles had just been using him to get an edge on the competition. Despite being in the middle of a crowd of people, Skip had never felt so alone.

## CHAPTER 6

# A SECOND CHANCE

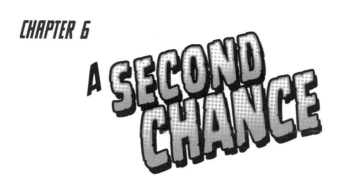

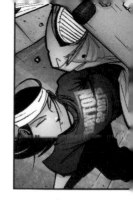

The following Saturday, Skip stayed in his room. It was the day of the regional tournament, but Skip didn't care. He was lying in bed, listening to music and reading issues of *SkateBoarder* magazine. Suddenly, he heard his mother calling him from downstairs.

"Skip! You have a visitor," she yelled.

Skip went downstairs to see who was there. To his surprise, Drew was standing in the doorway.

"Hey," Skip said.

"Hey," Drew replied. The two boys stood awkwardly in the doorway, avoiding eye contact. After a few moments, Drew broke the silence.

"Look, I'll get straight to the point," he said.

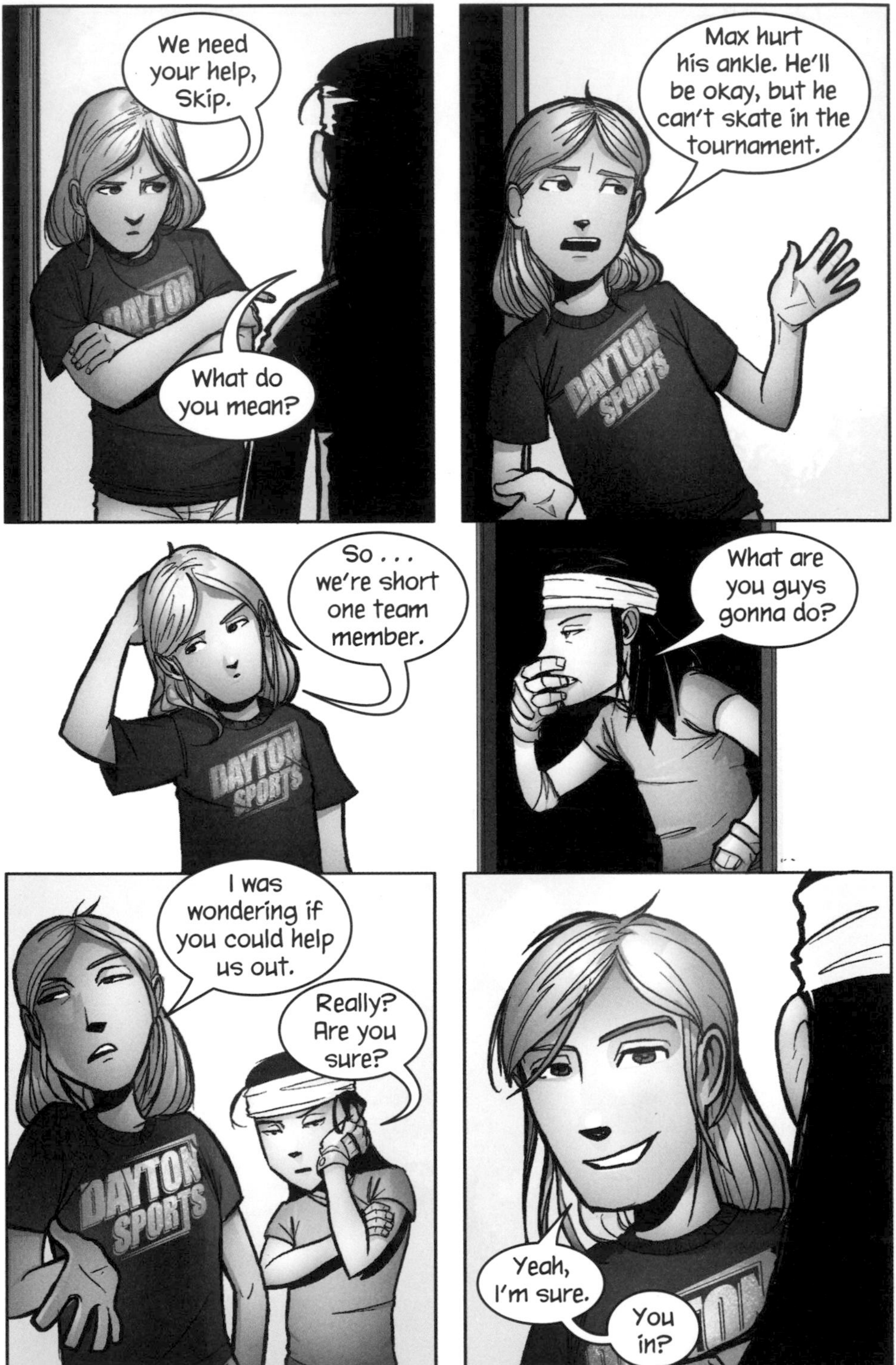
We need your help, Skip.
What do you mean?
Max hurt his ankle. He'll be okay, but he can't skate in the tournament.
So . . . we're short one team member.
What are you guys gonna do?
I was wondering if you could help us out.
Really? Are you sure?
Yeah, I'm sure.
You in?

Skip had spent all week trying to forget about the tournament. But he couldn't let his friends down. Not again.

Skip smiled. "Let me get my board," he said.

"All right!" Drew said. "Let's get going!"

Drew's father drove the two boys to the tournament. When they arrived, Max and Donnie were waiting for them. Max didn't look happy. As they walked over to the warm-up area, he pulled Skip aside. "Just so you know, I don't trust you," Max told Skip.

"I understand," Skip said. Then he added, "I really am sorry, Max. About your injury, about hanging with the Eagles — everything."

Max's face relaxed a little. "Yeah? Well, thanks," he said. "Just do me one favor, okay?"

"Anything," Skip replied.

"Get out there and destroy those Eagles!" Max said.

"You got it, buddy!" Skip said, as they slapped hands.

The first event of the competition was the slalom. Contestants from each team were paired up and had to race each other down the course. Skip won his first race easily. Then he lined up against the winner from another race and smoked him, too. Skip felt unbeatable.

As Skip walked up the ramp for the final race, he was surprised to find Joey waiting for him.

"Hey, buddy," Joey said with a sneer.

"Hey," Skip said.

"So I see you're back with those losers from Dayton Sports. It'll be my pleasure to smoke you in front of them," Joey said, loud enough that Max could hear him.

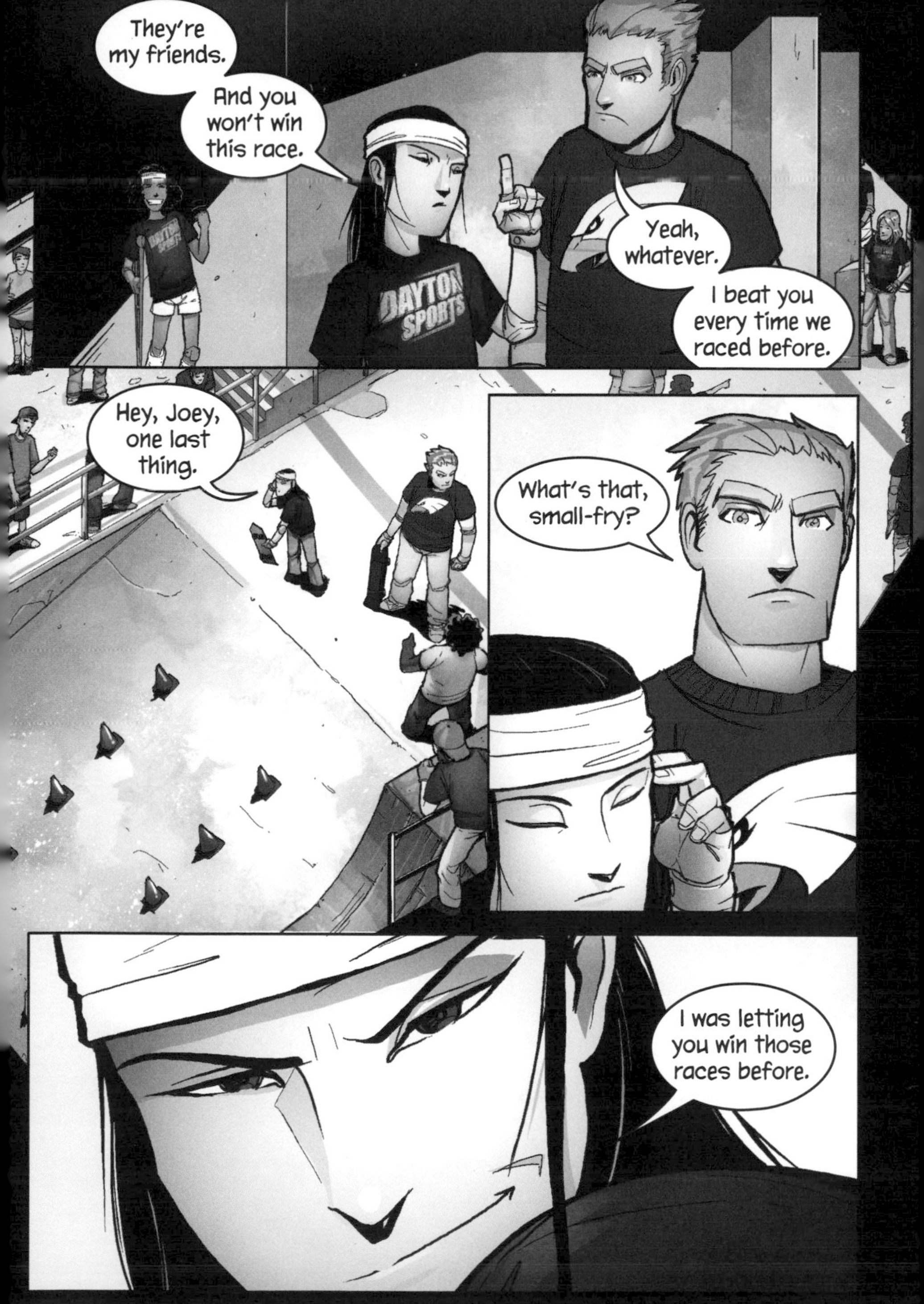
They're my friends.
And you won't win this race.
Yeah, whatever.
I beat you every time we raced before.
Hey, Joey, one last thing.
What's that, small-fry?
I was letting you win those races before.

"Oh, yeah?" Joey said, looking a little rattled. "We'll see about that, Skippy."

When the starter gun went off, Joey and Skip tipped their boards and raced down the ramp. They were neck and neck as they zigged and zagged through the orange cones. Skip tried to stay calm, crouching down on his board and leaning into every turn. Joey stayed with him, however, and the two boys battled their way to the bottom.

Then, just as they passed the last cone, Skip dropped as low as he could, pulling his knees into his chest and pushing his feet hard against his board. When they finally crossed the finish line, Skip had pulled ahead of Joey by the length of his board.

Max and Donnie were waiting for Skip at the bottom of the ramp.

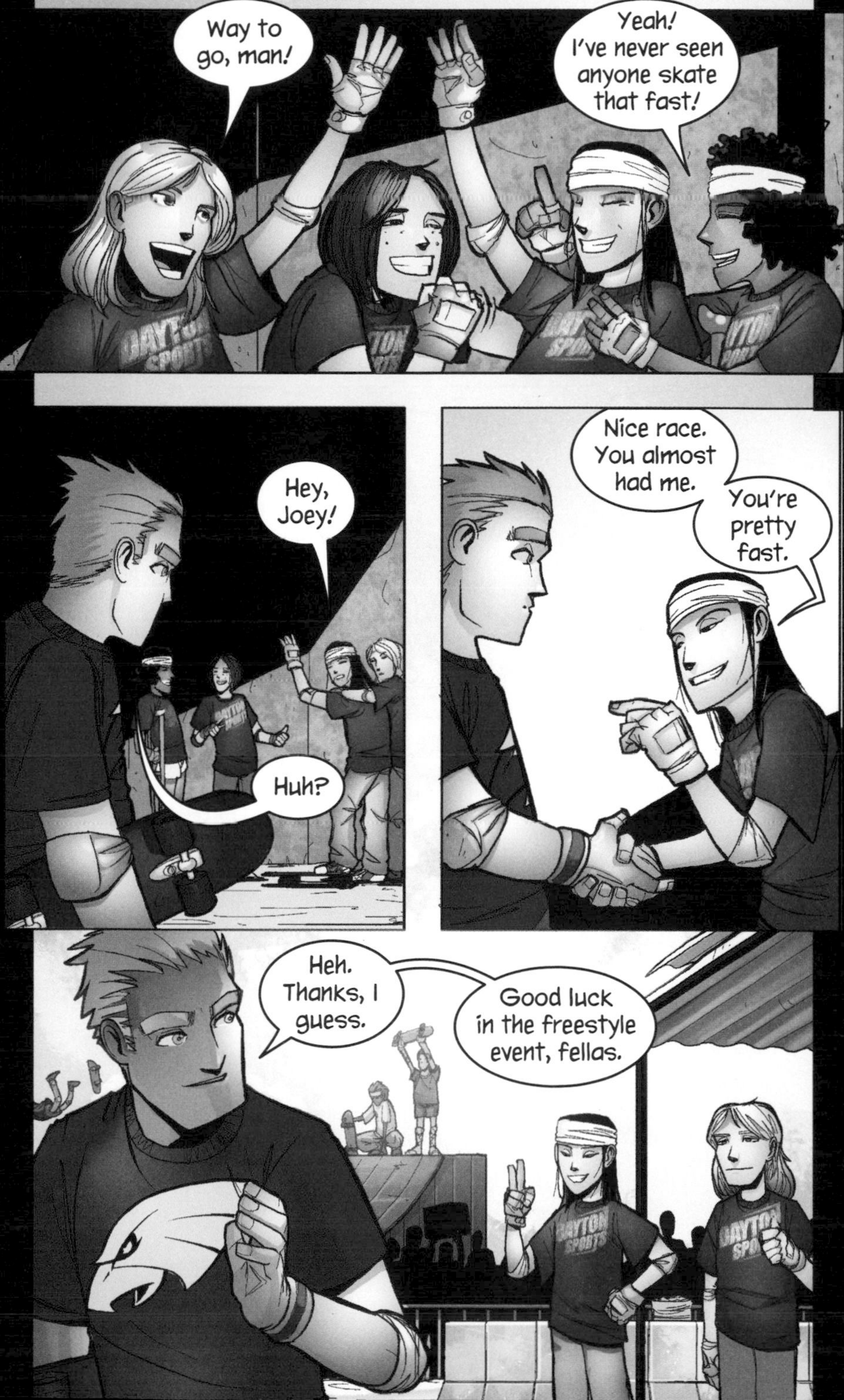
Way to go, man!
Yeah! I've never seen anyone skate that fast!
DAYTON SPORTS
Hey, Joey!
Huh?
Nice race. You almost had me.
You're pretty fast.
Heh. Thanks, I guess.
Good luck in the freestyle event, fellas.
DAYTON SPORTS

Soon, the judges for the freestyle event arrived. Some kids started whispering. As Skip looked up, he saw a familiar face.

"No way," Skip said. "Look who the second judge is!"

"It's Tony Alva!" Drew said. "I bet he'll like your style, Skip. You know, considering he helped create it!" Drew grinned widely.

Skip smiled back at Drew. "Good point," he said. "I'll keep that in mind."

The three boys sat and watched the other teams perform their freestyle routines. Soon, the Eagles took to the stage to perform their routine.

Skip couldn't watch. He waited for them to finish before turning around to see the scoreboard. To his dismay, he turned just in time to see Tony Alva nodding in approval. The Eagles received straight 9.9 scores — the highest so far in the competition.

"Don't worry," Drew said as he headed to the ramp. "We can beat them."

Drew stepped up to the ramp. He sped down and spun into a 360, then switched directions and spun into another. He did this several more times, switching back and forth each time. Then he kicked his board forward and balanced on its front wheels, tipping the back wheels off the ground. Then Drew slid backward, switching positions, balancing only on his back wheels. Skip was impressed. He had never seen Drew practice that trick before.

Finally, it was Skip's turn to perform.

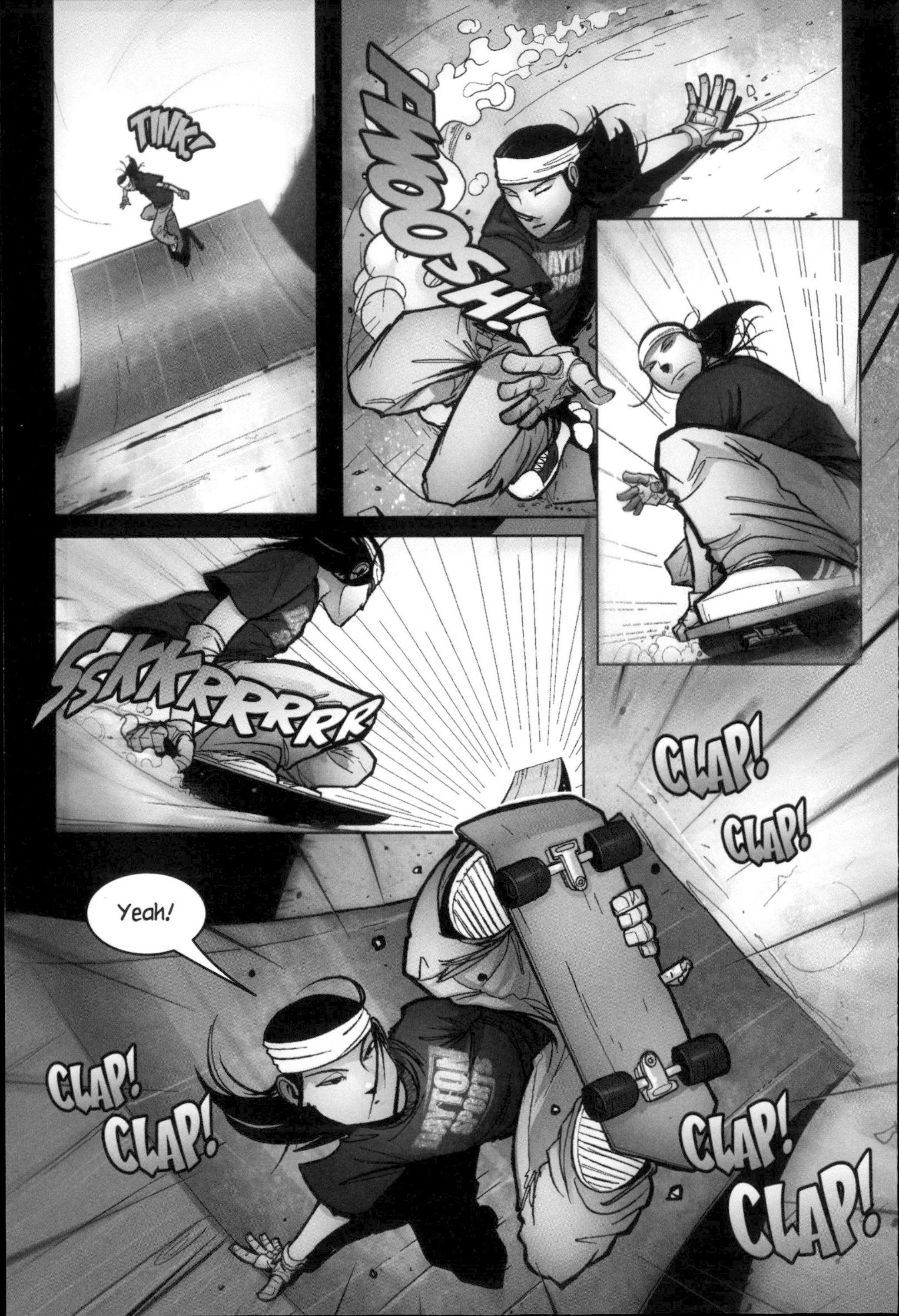
TINK!
FWOOSH!
SSKKRRRRRR
CLAP!
CLAP!
Yeah!
CLAP!
CLAP!
CLAP!
CLAP!

The crowd of cheering spectators never left their feet during Skip's routine. When he walked past the judge's table, he heard Alva tell the other judges, "That kid has some nice moves."

Skip couldn't believe it. His tricks had impressed one of the greatest skateboarders ever.

"Wow, that was awesome," said Drew, as he ran over to Skip. "But a handstand? I thought you said handstands were too old-fashioned."

"Yeah," agreed Max. "And what was with all those 360s? You said they were boring!"

"Well, maybe I was wrong," Skip said. "Sometimes you have to mix the old with the new. A good friend taught me that."

As Skip turned to look at his scores, he saw Tony Alva grinning at him. He was holding a scorecard with a perfect 10 above his head.

**THE 1970s:** A drought hits California, drying up most outdoor pools. For the first time, the Z-Boys drop in and skate the empty bowls.

**1973:** Jeff Ho, Skip Engblom, and Craig Stacy open the "Jeff Ho Surfboards and Zephyr Productions" store in Venice Beach.

**1973:** The Zephyr surf and skateboard team, known as the Z-Boys, is formed to promote the Zephyr surfing company. Tony Alva, Jay Adams, and Stacy Peralta join the team.

**1975:** Peggi Oki is the first and only female to join the Z-Boys team.

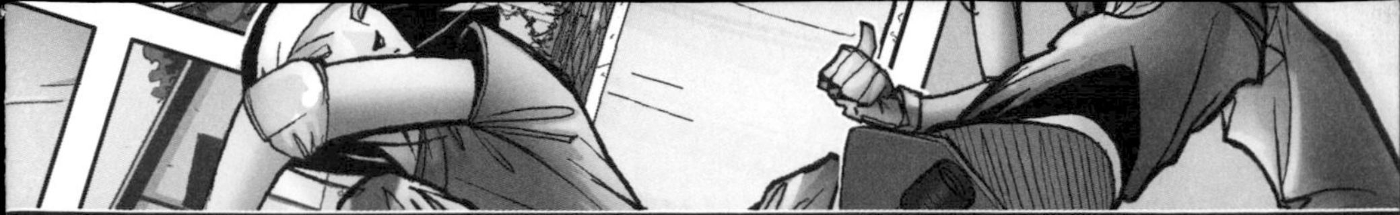

*1975:* The Z-Boys skating team debuts at the Del Mar Internationals. Judges have never seen anything like them before, and they don't know how to score their routines. Half of the finalists end up being Z-Boys.

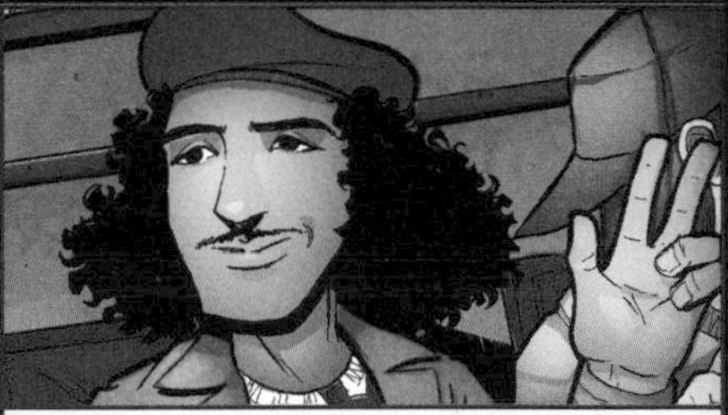

*1977:* Tony Alva becomes the first World Champion of Professional Skateboarding. He also sets the Guinness World Record for barrel jumping on a skateboard.

*2001:* A documentary entitled *Dogtown and the Z-Boys* is released to critical acclaim. The film chronicles the story of the Z-Boys. It is directed by Stacy Peralta, an original Z-Boy.

*2004:* A new skateboarding movie based on the Z-Boys is filmed. Stacy Peralta, original Z-Boy, wrote the screenplay.

# ABOUT THE AUTHOR

Xavier W. Niz grew up surfing the asphalt of New York City. After graduating from high school, he retired his board to pursue other interests, including college and eventually a job in publishing. However, the desire to ride came back while researching and writing *Drop In To the Deep End.* Xavier is currently learning how to ride a long board, and, more importantly, trying not to break anything while doing it.

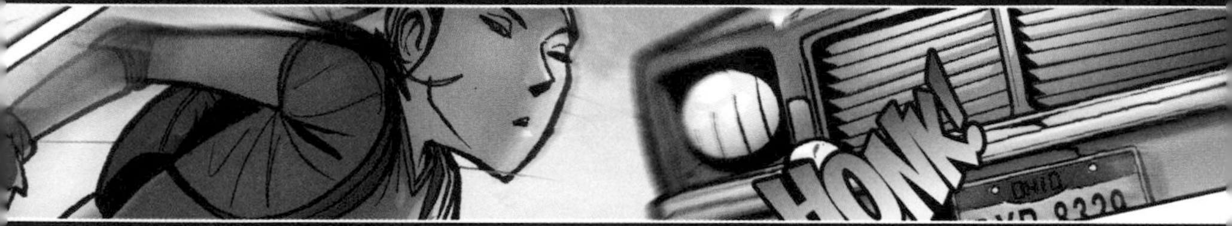

HONK


# ABOUT THE ILLUSTRATOR

Jesus Aburto was born in Monterrey, Mexico, in 1978. He has been a graphic designer, a colorist, and a freelance illustrator. Aburto has colored popular comic book characters for Marvel Comics and DC Comics, such as Wolverine, Ironman, Blade, and Nightwing. In 2008, Aburto joined Protobunker Studio, where he enjoys working as a comic book illustrator.

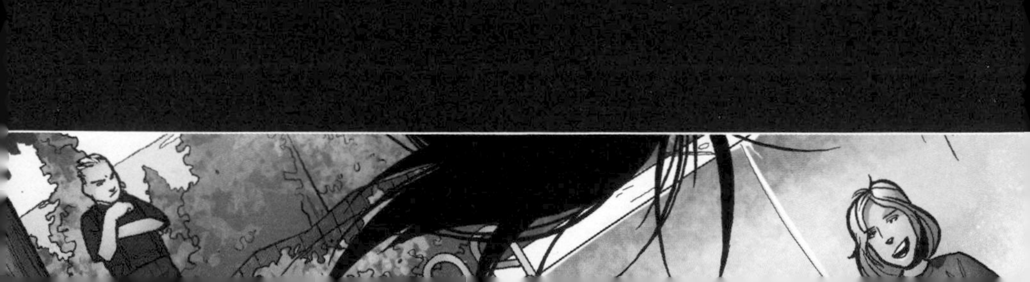

# GLOSSARY

awkwardly (AWK-wurd-lee)—if you are behaving awkwardly, you feel uncomfortable or uneasy

devoted (di-VOH-tid)—gave time, effort, and attention to something

dismay (diss-MAY)—distress or worry

emblazoned (em-BLAY-zuhnd)—decorated with colors and markings

flashy (FLASH-ee)—outlandish or fancy

sponsor (SPON-sur)—a person who gives money or support to a team that is competing in something

# DISCUSSION QUESTIONS

1. Half of this book is a traditional novel, and the other half is a graphic novel. Which part of this book did you like more?

2. Skip's mom yells at him for playing his music too loud. What do you do that upsets your family members?

3. Each page of a graphic novel has several illustrations called panels. Which panel in this book is your favorite? Why?

# WRITING PROMPTS

1. Skip hurt his teammate's feelings by abandoning them for the Eagles. When was the last time you hurt someone's feelings? What happened? How did it make you feel? Write about it.

2. Tony Alva and the Z-Boys are Skip's idols. Who are your role models? Why do you admire them? Write about the influence your favorite role model has had on your life.

3. At the end of the book, Skip scores a perfect 10 on his skating routine. What happens next? Does he get to hang out with his idol, Tony Alva? Does his team win the tournament? You decide.

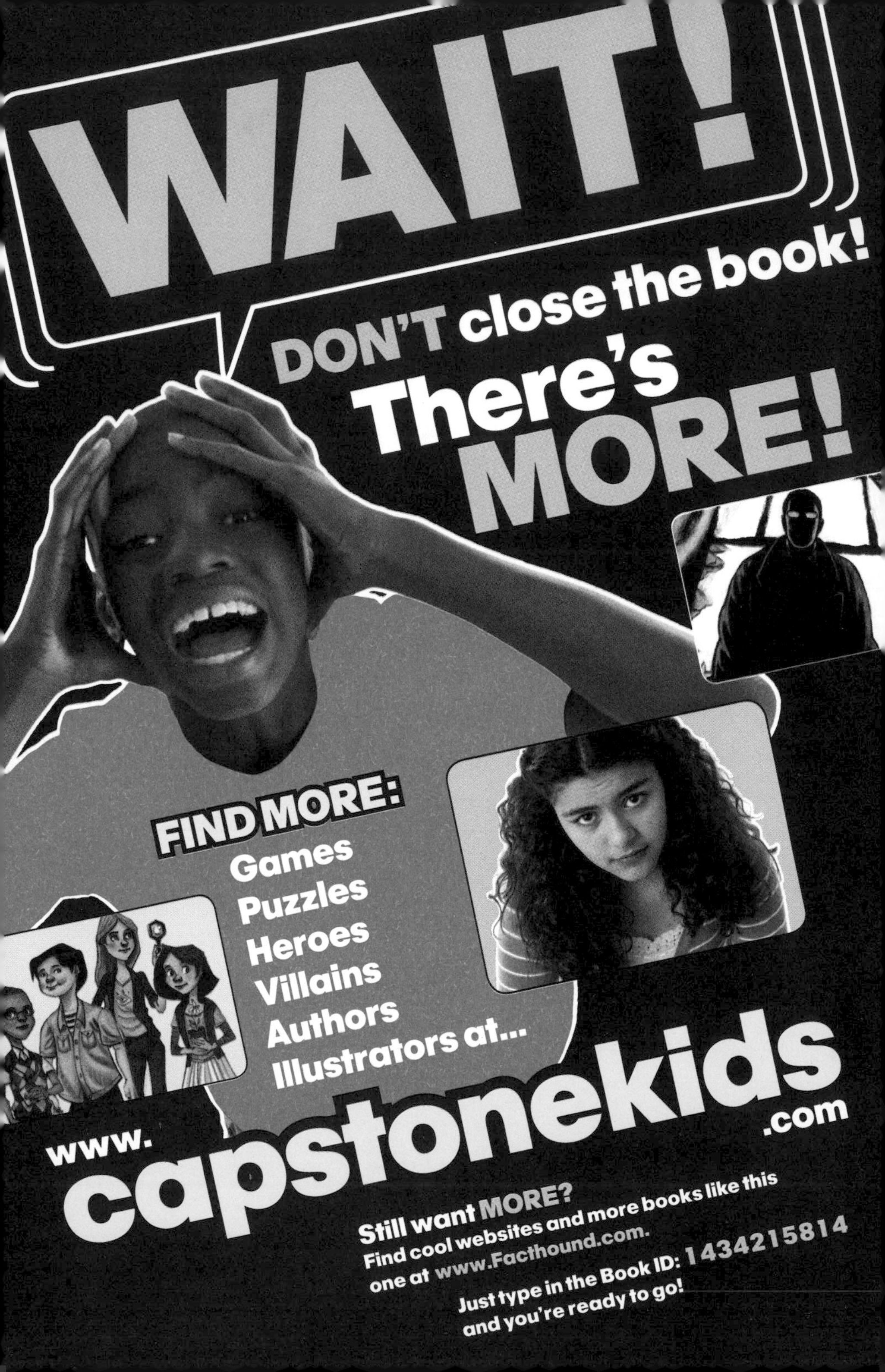
WAIT!
DON'T close the book!
There's MORE!
FIND MORE:
Games
Puzzles
Heroes
Villains
Authors
Illustrators at...
www.capstonekids.com
Still want MORE?
Find cool websites and more books like this one at www.Facthound.com.
Just type in the Book ID: 1434215814
and you're ready to go!